Barbie™

Stories
to
Share

Stories to Share

Cover photography by Joe Dias, Shirley Ushirogata,
Greg Roccia, Bill Coutts, Judy Tsuno, and Lisa Collins

 A GOLDEN BOOK • NEW YORK

BARBIE and associated trademarks and trade dress are owned by, and used under license from, Mattel, Inc.
Compilation copyright © 2004 Mattel, Inc. All Rights Reserved.
Published in the United States by Golden Books, an imprint of Random House Children's Books, a division of Random House, Inc., New York, and simultaneously in Canada by Random House of Canada Limited, Toronto.
No part of this book may be reproduced or copied in any form without permission from the copyright owner.
Golden Books, A Golden Book, and the G colophon are registered trademarks of Random House, Inc.
Library of Congress Control Number: 2004101248   ISBN: 0-375-82758-7
www.goldenbooks.com   MANUFACTURED IN CHINA   10 9 8 7 6 5 4 3 2 1

This collection comprises the following titles:

Summer Horse Camp
By Kristin Earhart. Illustrated by S.I. Artists. Copyright © 2002 Mattel, Inc. All Rights Reserved.

Horse Trouble!
By Kristin Earhart. Illustrated by S.I. Artists. Copyright © 2002 Mattel, Inc. All Rights Reserved.

A Big Bed for Me!
By Ann Braybrooks. Illustrated by S.I. International. Copyright © 2000 Mattel, Inc. All Rights Reserved.

I Got So Mad!
By Jean Bay. Illustrated by S.I. International. Copyright © 1999 Mattel, Inc. All Rights Reserved.

My First Day at Preschool
By Jean Bay. Illustrated by S.I. International. Copyright © 1999 Mattel, Inc. All Rights Reserved.

No More Mess!
By Ann Braybrooks. Illustrated by S.I. International. Copyright © 1999 Mattel, Inc. All Rights Reserved.

The New Baby
By Debra Mostow Zakarin. Illustrated by S.I. Artists. Copyright © 1998 Mattel, Inc. All Rights Reserved.

CONTENTS

Summer Horse Camp

By Kristin Earhart
Illustrated by S.I. Artists

It was the first day of camp. Stacie was really excited. She knew this summer at the Lucky Horseshoe Camp would be extra fun. Her sister Barbie was going to be her counselor and riding trainer.

Stacie walked over to the stables. There she saw a girl petting one of the horses.

"Hi! My name is Stacie. Are you here for horse camp?" Stacie asked.

"Yes," the girl said. "I'm Leslie. I've never ridden before."

"I rode Happy last year," Stacie said. "She's very gentle."

"I hope I get to ride a horse like Happy," said Leslie.

"There are other nice horses, but Happy's the best," Stacie said. "And I'm going to ride her."

"It's time to find out which horses you'll be riding," Barbie called to the campers.

Barbie read from a list. "Stacie will ride RC," she said. "Leslie will ride Happy,...."

"Barbie, why can't I ride Happy?" Stacie asked when Barbie was done reading from the list. "I was really good with her last year."

"Leslie is a beginner, so Happy is a good horse for her," Barbie explained. "Also, you'll be a better rider if you learn how to handle other horses."

Stacie went to the stables to meet RC. He was bigger than Happy. And Stacie had barely put her feet into the stirrups when RC threw his head in the air and started to prance sideways.

Stacie didn't know what to do. Then she remembered she had to be confident, so she pulled on the reins and nudged RC forward.

"Hi, Stacie," Leslie called. "Can you show me how to get on Happy?"

"I'm busy with RC right now, so I can't help you," Stacie replied. Then she clicked her tongue and trotted away on RC.

After classes, Stacie went to talk to her sister.

"RC is hyper," Stacie complained. "And he doesn't always listen to me."

"But I see you're doing a good job with him," Barbie said with a smile. "Now that you're an advanced rider, how about giving Leslie some advice?"

"But Happy is easy to ride," Stacie argued. "You said so yourself."

"Is that what you thought after your very first lesson?" Barbie asked.

"I guess not," Stacie said, remembering the tough time she'd had with Happy.

Stacie found Leslie and told her about the first year she was at camp. Then Stacie promised to help Leslie.

"You know," said Stacie, "I've been thinking about starting up a horse club. Would you like to be a member?"

"Cool!" Leslie said. "We could call it The Horseshoe Club."

"That's a great name," said Stacie. "Let's make up the club's goals together!"

The Horseshoe Club

1. Always help each other.
2. Learn as much as we can about horses.
3. Take care of our horses.
4. Help around the stable.

"On Friday, we'll have our big end-of-camp show,"
Barbie announced later that summer. "All of the campers
from the different cabins will compete."

Stacie and Leslie had been practicing every day, and
they couldn't wait for the show.

At the show, Stacie and Leslie both won ribbons for improving the most.

"I'm so proud of you two," Barbie said.

Both Stacie and Leslie were thrilled that they had won ribbons, but they were even more excited about their new club and new friendship.

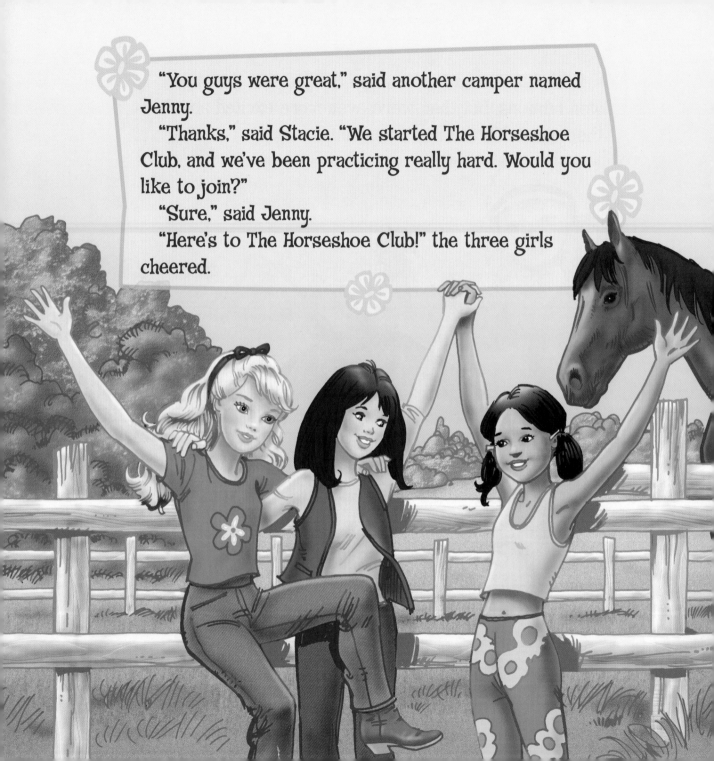

"You guys were great," said another camper named Jenny.

"Thanks," said Stacie. "We started The Horseshoe Club, and we've been practicing really hard. Would you like to join?"

"Sure," said Jenny.

"Here's to The Horseshoe Club!" the three girls cheered.

Horse Trouble!

By Kristin Earhart
Illustrated by S.I. Artists

"A new camper will be joining us today," Barbie said to the riders at the Lucky Horseshoe Camp. "I want you all to welcome Rebecca and her horse, Pixie."

"Wow," said Barbie's sister Stacie. "Rebecca's lucky that she gets to bring her own horse to camp."

Stacie didn't have her own horse. She rode RC, one of the camp's horses.

"Let's go say hello to Rebecca," Stacie said to her friends Leslie and Jenny.

"Hi. I'm Stacie and I ride RC," Stacie said to Rebecca. Rebecca didn't say anything. She kept brushing her horse's mane.

"Stacie, Jenny, and I are in The Horseshoe Club," Leslie said. "We go on trail rides and help around the stable. Would you like to join our club?"

Rebecca rolled her eyes. "I've been riding for three years," she said. "I know too much about riding to be in your little club. Now if you'll excuse me . . ."

Stacie, Leslie, and Jenny just looked at each other and shrugged.

Later that morning, Rebecca was upset because she had to take lessons with Stacie.

"But I don't want anyone holding me back," Rebecca said to Barbie.

"We always give group lessons," Barbie said. "You and Stacie will be good partners and have fun together."

Rebecca rode Pixie into the ring.

"Pixie is a really beautiful horse," Stacie complimented Rebecca.

"Thanks," Rebecca said. "I just got her for my birthday. We've already won first place at the fairground show," Rebecca declared. "We're perfect together."

Stacie didn't know what to say to Rebecca. After the lesson, Stacie asked Barbie if she and RC could take their next lesson with someone else.

"Stacie, you and Rebecca are at the same riding level," Barbie said. "Why don't you want to take your next lesson with her?"

"Rebecca is really good. She even won at the fairground show!" Stacie told Barbie. "And Pixie is perfect."

"But RC really trusts you. You two make a great team," Barbie said. "And that's more important than winning ribbons."

Stacie thought about how hard she and RC had worked. And she remembered all the fun they'd had with the other Horseshoe Club members.

"You're right. We are a good team, aren't we?"
Stacie said as she gave RC a hug. "I do care more
about that than ribbons and shows."

When it was time for their next lesson, Stacie was not as nervous. Stacie now knew she was just as good a rider as Rebecca.

During the lesson, a nearby car started honking suddenly. Its loud noise scared the horses. Stacie felt RC's body jolt with fear. She tightened the reins and spoke to him softly to try to calm him down.

Pixie was so frightened by the car's honking that she started to run out of the ring. Rebecca tried to hold on, but she soon fell out of her saddle. The honking stopped, but Pixie had already run into the stable.

"Are you okay?" asked Barbie and Stacie.

"I'm fine," Rebecca blushed. "Pixie always freaks out at loud noises."

"She's scared," Barbie said. "She'll get better as she learns to trust you."

"She'd better!" Rebecca said gruffly as she headed toward the stable.

"You were great, Stacie," Jenny said as she and Leslie ran up to her. "RC really listened to you."

"RC is a great horse," Stacie replied.

"And you're a great rider," Barbie said.

"Thanks, Barbie," Stacie said. "I'm glad RC trusts me. I wouldn't trade that for all the world."

Barbie™

My Feelings
Series

A Big Bed for Me!

By Ann Braybrooks
Illustrated by S.I. International

It's almost time for bed. But my friend Barbie is coming over. She lives nearby.

"I brought you something special!" Barbie says.

She gives me
a huge box with
a red ribbon.
I can't wait
to open it.

Inside the box is a big teddy bear. I can hardly wrap my arms around him! But I hug him as tightly as I can.

"Thank you, Barbie," I say.

"You're welcome," she says. "It's a big bear for a big girl!"

Barbie asks, "What are you
going to name him?"
I know the perfect name.
"I'm going to call him
Big Bear!"
"Let's go see how he likes
your room," Barbie says.

Big Bear is so big he doesn't fit into my crib. Where's he going to sleep?

There's a new big bed in my room. I wonder if he would like to sleep in it. The new bed is for me, but I haven't tried it out yet.

I put Big Bear in my new bed. The bed is *very* big. "Do you think Big Bear will be lonely?" I ask Barbie. "I don't think so," says Barbie. "But we can put these other animals and dolls next to him." Big Bear looks happy.

"What if Big Bear falls out?"
I ask Barbie.

"Well, I don't think that
will happen," says Barbie.
"But we can put this pillow
next to the bed, just in case."

The pillow is soft like
Big Bear.

I start to climb into the bed. If Big Bear can sleep in the bed, so can I. But then I stop.

"What if something jumps on the bed in the night?" I ask Barbie.

"Don't worry. Nothing will jump on the bed," says Barbie. "But your parents will always be nearby in case you need them."

"What if Big Bear can't see in the dark on this big bed?" I ask Barbie.

"We'll leave the hall light on," says Barbie. "Then Big Bear can see even when it's dark."

"What if Big Bear gets scared in the middle of the night anyway?" I ask.

"Then you can hug him and tell him everything will be all right." replies Barbie.

Barbie helps
me into the big bed.
Wow! It's easier
to get into than
my crib! She tucks
me under the covers.

Then Barbie tells me a bedtime story. It's about a little girl, just like me, who gets a new big bed and gets to sleep in it for the first time. The little girl is scared, but then she tries it out and it's not so bad.

"Good night," says Barbie.
She kisses me on the forehead
and blows Big Bear a kiss!
Then she leaves.

My new bed is big. But my
parents are close by. And Barbie
is nearby, too.

At first, I cannot sleep. Then I
think about the little girl in the
story. She was brave in her new big
bed. And she didn't even have
Big Bear to keep her company!

Now I feel sleepy. I look at Big Bear. He is falling asleep.
Big Bear likes my new bed! I like my new bed, too.

I Got So Mad!

By Jean Bay
Illustrated by S.I. International

Barbie was taking my class to the park. It was my turn to walk with her. I showed her my new pink bucket and shovel. "I'm going to make you a great big sandcake!" I said. "That sounds yummy!" said Barbie.

When we got to the park, I ran to the sandbox.
I filled my bucket with sand and turned it upside down.

"I'm going to make Barbie the best sandcake in the whole wide world," I thought to myself.

"One, two, three!" I yelled, and I lifted my bucket.

But I didn't have a sandcake. I just had a slippery-slidey
pile of sand.

I tried again.
And again.
And again.

But all I made were slippery-slidey sandpiles.
I didn't make even one sandcake!

A little boy came up to me. "Why are you making those
dumb old piles of sand?" he asked.

A red hot feeling started in my tummy.

"They're not dumb old sandpiles," I said.
"They're sandcakes for Barbie!"
　"Are not!" the boy said.
　"Are too!" I shouted.
　The red hot feeling got bigger and bigger.

It got so big that, all of a sudden, I made a mean face right at that boy.

"I'm telling Barbie!" he yelled. And he ran away.

And then the red hot feeling popped right out of my mouth.
"AAAAAHH!" I yelled.

"These *are* dumb sandpiles!" I yelled. I jumped up
and down on them. "And this is a dumb bucket!" I shouted.
I threw my dumb bucket as hard as I could.

My bucket went up, up, up. Then it came down, down, down. It landed in a tree. A BIG tree! Now I was mad all over.

My feet were mad, and my arms were mad. I was hot and sticky, and my face felt icky. And I couldn't stop being mad.

Barbie ran up and hugged me. "Take a nice long breath," she said. "Then use your words to tell me what's wrong." The red hot feeling got a little bit smaller.

"I tried to make sandcakes for you," I said. "But I just made sandpiles. And now my bucket is gone!"

"What do you want to have happen right now?" Barbie asked. "And if you can't do it by yourself, can you ask for help?"

I took a deep breath. "I want my bucket back," I said. "Can you help me?"

Barbie lifted me up to get my bucket. Then we got water from the drinking fountain to make wet sand. The red hot feeling was almost all gone.

I put the wet sand in my bucket. Then I turned the bucket upside down. When I lifted it up, out came the best sandcake in the whole wide world!

"Yummy!" said Barbie.

And I was glad all over.

My First Day at Preschool

By Jean Bay
Illustrated by S.I. International

Tomorrow is my first day of preschool.

I have a new lunch box and new pink sneakers.

Mama says school is fun.

But I am not sure I want to go. Neither is Rocky.

He's my bunny.

Rocky and I went next door to show my new sneakers to my friend Barbie.

"I'm going to school tomorrow," I told her.

"You'll make lots of new friends," said Barbie.

"See you soon!" she said when I left.

But what if no one wants to be my friend? I wondered.

At lunchtime Mama let Rocky and me have a picnic
in the backyard.

"What if I get hungry at school?" I asked Rocky.
But Rocky didn't know.

After lunch I drew a picture of school with my new crayons. It was so big, I knew Rocky was wondering if I'd get lost inside.

I wondered about that, too.

That night, while I had my bath, I thought about school.
"What if I get my hands dirty, and I can't reach the sink
to wash them?" I whispered to Rocky. Rocky didn't know.

"And where do I go to get a drink if I'm thirsty?"
I asked Rocky. But Rocky didn't know that, either.

In the morning, Mama took me and Rocky to school. We walked through a pink door with a sign on it that said IN.

"Now I know where to go," I told Rocky. "Maybe I won't get lost after all."

Mama and Rocky and I went into a sunny room.
And there was Barbie!

"I told you we'd see each other soon!" she said.
"I'm your new teacher!" She hugged me and Rocky.
We hugged her back—really hard!

Barbie showed me a yellow table with four chairs.
"This is where you sit," she said.

The chair was just the right size for my feet to touch
the floor. I liked sitting in it.

A little girl with a teddy bear sat down beside me.
She smiled at me. I smiled back.

"Maybe she'll be a new friend," I whispered to Rocky.
He thought so, too.

Then Barbie gave me a smock to put on. It was just my size.

"Paint a picture of your favorite thing," said Barbie.

I painted a picture of Rocky.

But my fingers got sticky green and yellow paint all over them. Uh-oh, I thought.

Barbie took us all to the bathroom to wash our hands.
If I stood just a teensy bit on my tiptoes, I could reach
the sink just fine.

On the way back to our room, Barbie showed us the drinking fountains.

There was a big one for bigger kids. And there was one just the right size for me.

When we got back to the room, Barbie said, "Snacktime!" We got crackers and juice. They were good.

Then it was time to play outside.

We went on the swings. They were just the right size for me and my new friend.

And when it was time to go back inside, we found our room without getting lost at all!

Before I knew it, it was time to go home.

"See you tomorrow!" said Barbie.

I ran outside to meet my Mama. "You were right! School is fun," I told her.

I want to go back tomorrow.

And so does Rocky.

No More Mess!

By Ann Braybrooks
Illustrated by S.I. International

Oh no!
It just started to drizzle, and I can't find
my pink raincoat with the purple dots anywhere.
I looked in the family closet.
I looked in my room.
I even looked in the kitchen!

But I can't find it anywhere.
Just when I'm about to give up, Barbie comes over.
Maybe she can help me. But why is she laughing?
"Oh, Nina," she says. "Your room is such a mess!"

"But I like my room this way!" I tell Barbie.
"It's easy to find my toys when they're on the floor.
Now, if only I could find my raincoat."

Barbie walks over to a pile of stuff in the corner of my room. "Maybe your raincoat is hiding under here."

While Barbie watches, I look through all my stuff.
I find dolls, stuffed animals, books, and toys.
When I get to the bottom, I say, "See? No raincoat!"
    But I do find my pink ballet slippers. It's too bad I didn't know
where they were this morning when I wanted to practice ballet.
I was pretty sad about that.

"Maybe we'll find your raincoat in another room," says Barbie.

I follow her into the living room. "I already looked here," I tell her.

"It doesn't hurt to look again," says Barbie.

We look, but not for long. The living room is so neat.
We don't have to dig for stuff like I do in my room.

Oh look! There's my pink tutu under the couch.
It's been lost for a week!

Next we look in all the other rooms in the house.
And in all the closets. "We'll never find my coat!"

"Let's try your room again," says Barbie. "But first,
I want to show you something. Let's grab an umbrella
and go to my house for a minute."

Barbie shows me her bedroom. It's pretty, but where is all her stuff?

"I got tired of looking for my things all the time," says Barbie. "So I found places to store them. See?"

Barbie pulls out two baskets from a shelf. One is filled with scarves. The other is filled with belts.

All of Barbie's books are placed neatly on the shelves, too.

Then Barbie opens her closet.
Wow! Everything is so neat!
Stacked on the shelves are a bunch of clear plastic boxes.
One box has cards and letters from her friends. One box has purses.
And another one has some baseball caps, a baseball, and a mitt.
All of Barbie's clothes are hanging neatly on bars.
And her shoes are all lined up, too!

"I have some extra boxes and baskets," says Barbie.
"Would you like them? They might help you to organize
your things."

"Yes! Thank you!" I say.

Barbie and I carry the boxes and baskets back to my house.

We put all my stuff into boxes and baskets.
I place my books on my shelf the way I want them.
"But we still haven't found my raincoat," I say.
"Let's check your closet again," Barbie says.
"OK," I agree.

Next thing I know, we're cleaning up my closet!
And what do I find, buried beneath a whole bunch of junk?
My raincoat!
Barbie also finds my leotard!
Now I don't know whether to put on my raincoat and
go outside, or stay inside and practice ballet!

I decide to stay inside and be a ballerina! But just so
I can be sure to find my raincoat the next time I need it,
I hang it up neatly in the family closet where it belongs!
I've decided that I like it when I'm neat and there's
no more mess!

Dear
Barbie

The New Baby

By Debra Mostow Zakarin
Illustrated by S.I. Artists

Dear Barbie,
I have a new baby sister. Because they're so busy with her, my parents don't have as much time to play with me anymore. That makes me so sad! Have you ever felt this way?

Love,
Jessica

Barbie sat down to answer Jessica's letter. She wrote:

Dear Jessica,
It's difficult getting used to being a big sister. I've gone
through it and so have my sisters Skipper and Stacie. Skipper
felt jealous when Stacie was born. Then by the time Ashley
came along, Skipper was older and loved being a big sister. But
Stacie still had to get used to the idea.

Barbie continued her letter to Jessica, and this is the story
she told. . . .

Early one morning Barbie, Skipper, and Stacie were
admiring their baby sister, Ashley.

"Isn't she just the cutest baby you've ever seen?"
commented Barbie.

"I thought *I* was the cutest baby you'd ever seen,"
said Stacie.

"You *were*," said Skipper. "But you're a big girl now."
Stacie just turned and stormed out of the room.

Later that morning Stacie sat silently at the breakfast table while Barbie prepared a bottle for Ashley.

"Barbie," Stacie finally said, "do you think we could go somewhere together—just you and me?"

"Of course," said Barbie. "But I can't do it right now. I have to feed Ashley first."

"Oh," said Stacie, staring down at her cereal.

"I have an idea," said Barbie. "Why don't you help me?"

Stacie shook her head no. Without looking up she said, "I don't think so. I have other things to do."

"Okay," said Barbie gently. "I understand. Maybe later. And if you like, when Ashley's taking her nap, you and I can talk."

Barbie went into the family room to feed Ashley. After a moment, Skipper joined her. Then Stacie walked by and stood in the doorway.

"Want to go to the playground, Skipper?" she asked. "They have a new water slide there."

"I can't," said Skipper. "I promised to help bathe Ashley after she has her bottle."

"Why don't you help us, too," offered Barbie. "It could be fun!"

"No, I don't feel like it," said Stacie as she turned and walked away.

After Ashley's bath, Barbie and Skipper put her down for a nap. As they silently tiptoed out of the room, loud noises rang throughout the house.

"Look at me!" shouted Stacie, who was marching down the hall banging some cymbals together. "I'm a majorette!"

"Shhh!" said Barbie. "Ashley is napping!"

"Ashley! Ashley! Ashley!" shouted Stacie as she threw her cymbals down. "Nobody cares about me anymore!"

Stacie ran down the hallway and into her room. Barbie followed quickly after her.

"Of course we care about you," Barbie said gently.

"No you don't," sobbed Stacie. "You never even have time to play with me anymore!"

"Stacie, I know it's not easy having a new baby sister. Babies take a lot of time and hard work. But you're still just as special to us as you've always been," Barbie said. "No one could ever take your place."

Barbie handed Stacie a tissue. "Listen, Stacie," she continued. "When Ashley wakes up, why don't you and I take her to the park. Then we can talk some more."

Stacie thought for a moment. "Okay," she finally agreed.

As they walked, Stacie started to feel a bit better. "Look what I can do!" she said, turning a cartwheel.

"Stacie, that's wonderful!" said Barbie.

Ashley giggled. "Listen!" added Barbie. "Ashley likes it, too."

"You think so?" asked Stacie.

"I *know* so," said Barbie. "It reminds me of the way Skipper used to make you laugh when *you* were a baby."

"She did?" asked Stacie.

"Sure," said Barbie, "after she got used to having you around. It wasn't easy for her having a baby sister at first, either."

"Gee," said Stacie. "I guess not. I never thought of that before."

Barbie and Stacie began making plans to spend a special day together—just the two of them.

"Let's go shopping, out to lunch, and then to the movies!" said Stacie.

"Wow! All in one day? That sounds like fun!" exclaimed Barbie.

Just then Ashley started crying.

"I wonder what's wrong," said Barbie, picking her up. "We just fed and changed her. What do you think it could be?"

"I don't know," said Stacie. Then suddenly her face brightened. "Wait a minute!" she exclaimed. "I'll be right back." She turned and ran back down the path.

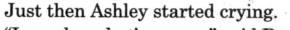

In a moment Stacie returned. "Here you go, Ashley!"
she said, handing her a pink toy. "You dropped your rattle.
Do you feel better now?"

Ashley smiled and waved the rattle at Stacie.

"Wow!" said Barbie. "What a smart big sister you are, Stacie! You knew exactly what was wrong!"

Stacie smiled proudly. "Yeah, I guess I did," she agreed.

Later that day, Barbie and Stacie sat relaxing in the living room.

"Am I holding her right?" asked Stacie.

"Perfect," said Barbie. "You really *are* a very good big sister, you know."

Stacie looked up at Barbie and smiled. Then she looked back down at Ashley. "And I have the best baby sister in the whole world," she added.

That evening, Barbie had some good news for Stacie. "I've put aside tomorrow just for you," she announced.

"Yippee!" said Stacie. Then she paused and looked over at Ashley. "Barbie," she said, "do you think that someday Ashley will want to have special days just with me?"

Ashley looked up at Stacie. "Yah, yah, yah!" she babbled.
"I guess so!" said Barbie. Then she and Stacie started
laughing—and baby Ashley joined in.

Barbie finished her letter to Jessica:

As you see, Stacie is just as important to our family as she ever was, and I'm sure you are to your family, too. But babies take lots of time and attention. So try to be patient. You'll start to see how much fun being a big sister can be.

Love,
Barbie

Which of these Barbie™ books have you read?

Based on the Video!

Storybooks

Padded Hardcover

Barbie Rules!

Barbie: Be Your Own Best Friend!

Barbie: Be Proud of Yourself!

Barbie: No Teasing Allowed!

STEP INTO READING®

Learning to Read, Step by Step!

STEP INTO READING — Level 1 — Barbie School Days

STEP INTO READING — Level 1 — Barbie One Pink Shoe

STEP INTO READING — Level 2 — Barbie On the Road

a *Little Golden Book*®

A FAIRY TALE — Barbie Cinderella

A BALLET STORY — Barbie The Nutcracker

Barbie Sleeping Beauty

Barbie Swan Lake

www.randomhouse.com/kids
www.goldenbooks.com

RANDOM HOUSE CHILDREN'S BOOKS

Golden Books®